3
5
Annie

EGMONT

We bring stories to life

First published in Great Britain in 2017
by Egmont UK Limited
The Yellow Building, 1 Nicholas Road, London W11 4AN

Thomas the Tank Engine & Friends™

CREATED BY BRITT ALLCROFT

Based on the Railway Series by the Reverend W Awdry

ISBN 978 1 4052 8770 8
67244/1
Printed in Italy

Written by Emily Stead. Designed by Claire Yeo.
Series designed by Martin Aggett.

This story is about what
happened one snowy winter.
Percy and I worked together
to make sure our friends in
the mountain village had
a happy Christmas . . .

One snowy Christmas Eve, The Fat Controller visited Thomas and Percy.

"Take Thomas' coaches and deliver the Christmas post to the village, please," he told Percy. "Thomas will help clear snow today."

Thomas was sad. "I won't be able to wish the villagers a happy Christmas," he frowned.

"Don't worry, I'll do it for you," Percy smiled.

Percy set off up the mountain with Annie and Clarabel. Snow wasn't going to slow **him** down!

Through the falling snowflakes, Percy saw a red glow ahead. When he got closer, he saw that it was a Fogman, holding up a warning light.

"Snow has blocked every road and track to the village," the Fogman called. "You must fetch help, Percy."

6

Percy had to help the villagers stuck in the snow. He thought of an idea. He left his carriages in a siding and steamed to see Harold at the Airport.

"**Peep! Peep!** Wake up!" whistled Percy. "The mountain villagers need our help."

"Right away!" Harold buzzed. And off he flew to tell The Fat Controller.

ROLD

On his way back to the Yard, Percy met Thomas.

The Fat Controller had received the call for help, and sent Thomas to take Terence the Tractor and a works train to help the villagers.

"Thank you for looking after my friends, Percy," puffed Thomas. "Now, follow me!"

Percy buffered up behind Thomas' heavy train, and they set off for the village. Thomas' snowplough cleared the tracks, but climbing the mountain was hard work.

Thomas and Percy had to go very slowly. When they tried to go faster, their wheels **slipped** and **spun** on the icy rails. But they kept going together.

Then at last, “There’s the village!” Thomas called.

Percy was very tired, but he **huffed** his hardest, until the train was safely in the station.

Just then, Percy heard a buzzing noise in the sky. It was Harold! He was dropping parcels of food for the villagers and their pets.

HAROLD

Then Terence got to work. With his strong caterpillar tracks and snowplough, he cleared the snow so that people could walk safely and drive their cars.

"Snow is super stuff!" chuffed Terence cheerfully.

The children thought so, too. They loved sledging down hills and making snowmen.

At last, the snowstorm passed. Terence ploughed the last road in the village, and rolled back onto Thomas' flatbed.

Percy went to fetch Annie and Clarabel from the siding. He still had all the Christmas post to deliver to the villagers!

By the time he returned, Toby had brought hot chocolate and mince pies for the tired workmen and villagers.

6
7

Soon, it was time for the engines to puff home.

"Well done, Percy! Well done, Thomas!" the villagers cheered and waved. "Thank you for giving us a happy Christmas!"

The engines smiled. They loved to be Really Useful!

When Thomas and Percy had gone, the villagers planned a special surprise to thank the engines.

That night, the villagers packed Toby's carriage full of parcels. Then Toby puffed through the snowy countryside to the Yard, as quietly as he could.

Thomas and Percy were fast asleep after their busy day. The villagers tiptoed into the Shed carrying the parcels. Toby wondered what the surprise was going to be.

1
7

Thomas gasped when he woke up on Christmas morning. **"Cinders and ashes!"** he smiled.

The Shed had been decorated with fairy lights and tinsel, and there was a real Christmas tree with presents underneath.

"What a magical Christmas!" said Percy.

"Surprises always make the best Christmas presents," Thomas peeped.

More about Terence

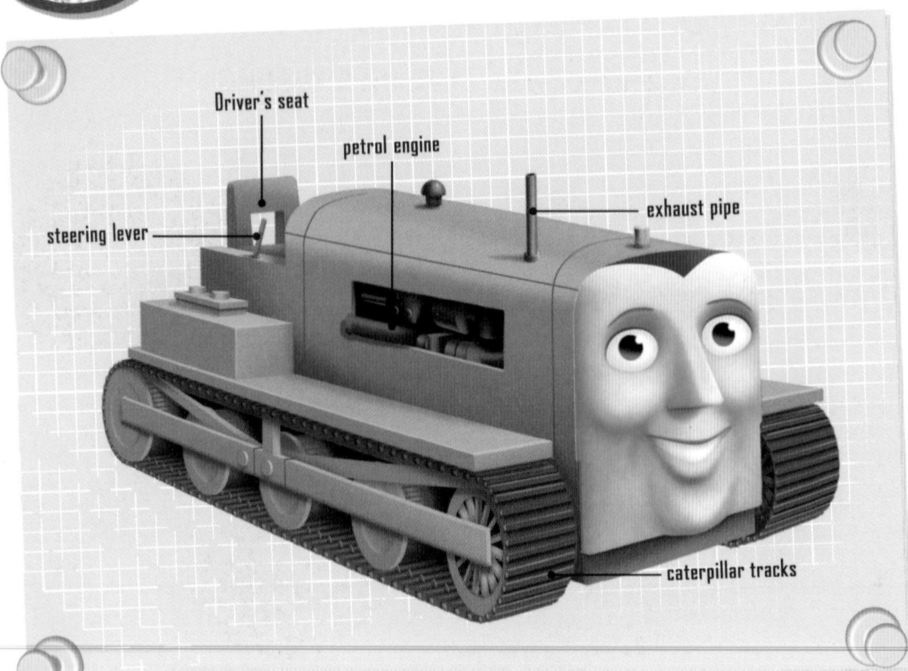

• Terence's challenge to you •

Look back through the pages of this book and see if you can spot:

3
5
Annie